# MR. RUDE

Roger Hargreaves

Written and illustrated by
Adam Hargreaves

Mr Rude is rude.

He is very rude.

He is very, very rude.

He is worse than very, very rude.

He is extraordinarily rude.

When you meet somebody, you might think to yourself that that person has a large nose, but you wouldn't say anything to them, would you?

Because that would be rude, wouldn't it?

Well, Mr Rude would just blurt it out.

"Big nose!"

But he wouldn't stop there.

Oh no, not Mr Rude.

"Big nose! With a nose like that you could vacuum the floor!"

Can you imagine saying that to someone?

Well, I hope you can't!

And he was the same with everyone.

If he met someone overweight he would shout, "Fatty! You're supposed to take the food out of the fridge, not eat the fridge as well!"

When he was driving along in his car he would yell rude things at the people he passed by.

Mr Rude was a horrible man who didn't have a nice thing to say to anyone and, not surprisingly, no-one liked him.

One day Mr Rude met Little Miss Tiny. (Or not so much met as nearly trod on her.)

"Good morning," said Little Miss Tiny.

"Look at the size of you!" exclaimed Mr Rude. "Squirt! You're so tiny I could squash you under my thumb!"

Poor Little Miss Tiny burst into tears and ran home.

Behind a tree on the other side of the lane Mr Happy looked anything but happy.

He had heard everything.

The next morning Mr Happy was outside Mr Rude's house, suitcase in hand.

Mr Happy knocked on Mr Rude's front door.

"Go away!" shouted Mr Rude.

Mr Happy knocked again.

Mr Rude opened the door.

"Can't you read," said Mr Rude, pointing to his doormat.

Mr Rude's doormat did not say 'welcome' like everyone else's doormat. Mr Rude had crossed out 'WELCOME' and then, in large black letters, had written 'GO AWAY!' underneath.

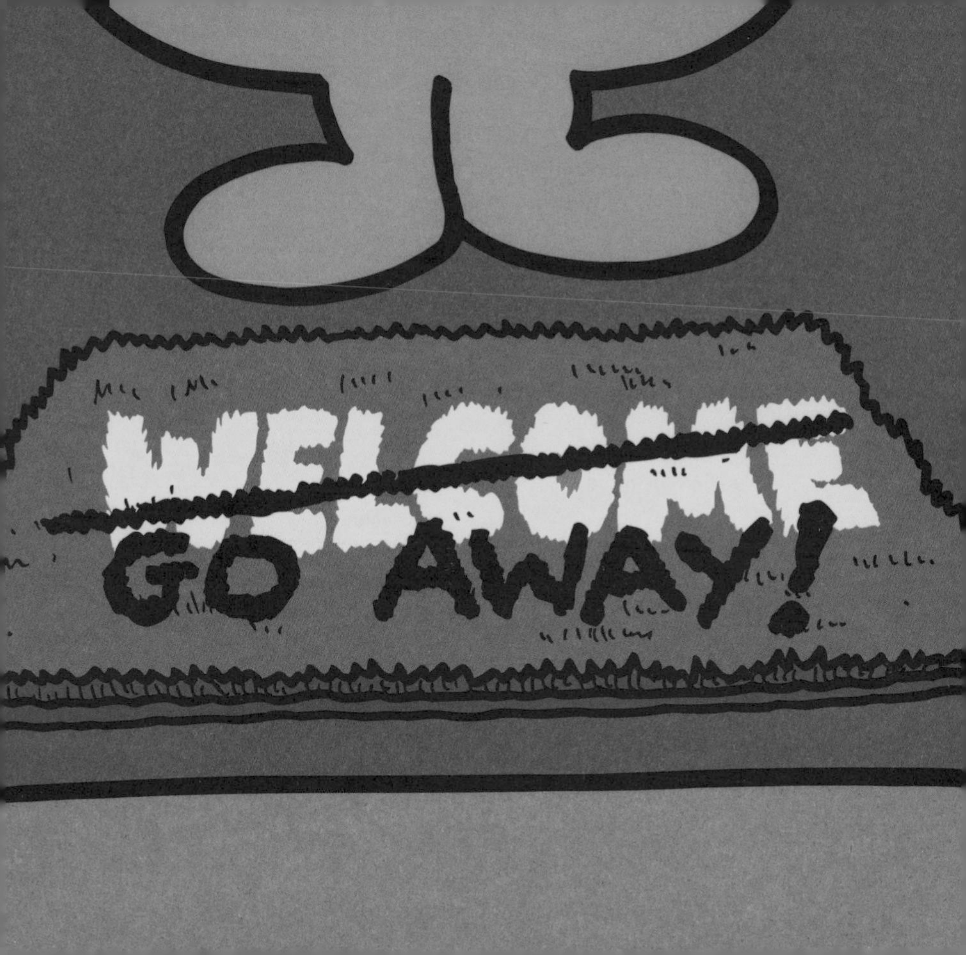
WELCOME
GO AWAY!

Mr Happy smiled, barged past Mr Rude and went into the living room.

"GET OUT!" shouted Mr Rude.

Mr Happy smiled an even larger smile and sat down in the armchair.

Mr Rude exploded. He ranted and raged for half an hour, but Mr Happy calmly sat through it all, smiling.

Eventually, Mr Rude went into the kitchen to make himself supper, without offering any to Mr Happy.

After his supper Mr Rude ranted and raged for a full hour, but, whatever Mr Rude called him, Mr Happy took no notice.

Finally, Mr Rude turned out the lights and went upstairs without offering Mr Happy a bed for the night.

When he came down in the morning Mr Happy was still there, still smiling.

"OK, I give in!" cried Mr Rude. "What do you want?"

"Breakfast would be nice," said Mr Happy. "Please."

Mr Rude made breakfast for him.

It was the first time in Mr Rude's life that he had ever done anything for someone else.

In fact, it was the first time he had ever asked anybody what they wanted.

"Thank you," said Mr Happy, when he had finished.

"Right! You can go now!" demanded Mr Rude.

But Mr Happy did not budge.

Mr Rude ranted and raged and raged and ranted, but he ended up making lunch for Mr Happy . . . and supper.

He even offered Mr Happy a bed that night.

Mr Happy stayed for a fortnight.

Slowly the ranting and raging became less and less.

Mr Rude discovered he had something that he had never known he possessed.

Manners!

When it was time for Mr Happy to leave he shook
Mr Rude's hand and said, "Thank you so much,
Mr Rude. I really enjoyed my stay."

Mr Rude beamed a smile that was every bit as wide as
Mr Happy's and found himself saying, "And so did I."

Mr Rude was a changed man.

"Burp!" belched Mr Rude.

Well, almost!

# Fantastic offers for Mr. Men fans!

**Collect all your Mr. Men or Little Miss books in these superb durable collectors' cases!**

Only £5.99 inc. postage and packing, these wipe-clean, hard-wearing cases will give all your Mr. Men or Little Miss books a beautiful new home!

**Keep track of your collection with this giant-sized double-sided Mr. Men and Little Miss Collectors' poster.**

Collect 6 tokens and we will send you a brilliant giant-sized double-sided collectors' poster! Simply tape a £1 coin to cover postage and packaging in the space provided and fill out the form overleaf.

**STICK £1 COIN HERE** (for poster only)

**Only need a few Mr. Men or Little Miss to complete your set?** You can order any of the titles on the back of the books from our Mr. Men order line on 0870 787 1724. Orders should be delivered between 5 and 7 working days.

--- TO BE COMPLETED BY AN ADULT ---

To apply for any of these great offers, ask an adult to complete the details below and send this whole page with the appropriate payment and tokens, to: MR. MEN CLASSIC OFFER, PO BOX 715, HORSHAM RH12 5WG

☐ Please send me a giant-sized double-sided collectors' poster.
AND ☐ I enclose 6 tokens and have taped a £1 coin to the other side of this page.

☐ Please send me ☐ Mr. Men Library case(s) and/or ☐ Little Miss library case(s) at £5.99 each inc P&P
☐ I enclose a cheque/postal order payable to Egmont UK Limited for £.................
OR ☐ Please debit my MasterCard / Visa / Maestro / Delta account (delete as appropriate) for £.................

Card no. ☐☐☐☐ ☐☐☐☐ ☐☐☐☐ ☐☐☐☐ ☐☐☐☐ ☐☐☐☐    Security code ☐☐☐

Issue no. (if available) ☐    Start Date ☐☐/☐☐/☐☐    Expiry Date ☐☐/☐☐/☐☐

Fan's name: ...................................    Date of birth: ...................................

Address: ...................................

...................................

Postcode: ...................................

Name of parent / guardian: ...................................

Email for parent / guardian: ...................................

Signature of parent / guardian: ...................................

Please allow 28 days for delivery. Offer is only available while stocks last. We reserve the right to change the terms of this offer at any time and we offer a 14 day money back guarantee. This does not affect your statutory rights. Offers apply to UK only.

☐ We may occasionally wish to send you information about other Egmont children's books.
If you would rather we didn't, please tick this box.

**Ref: MRM 001**

cut along the dotted line and return this whole page